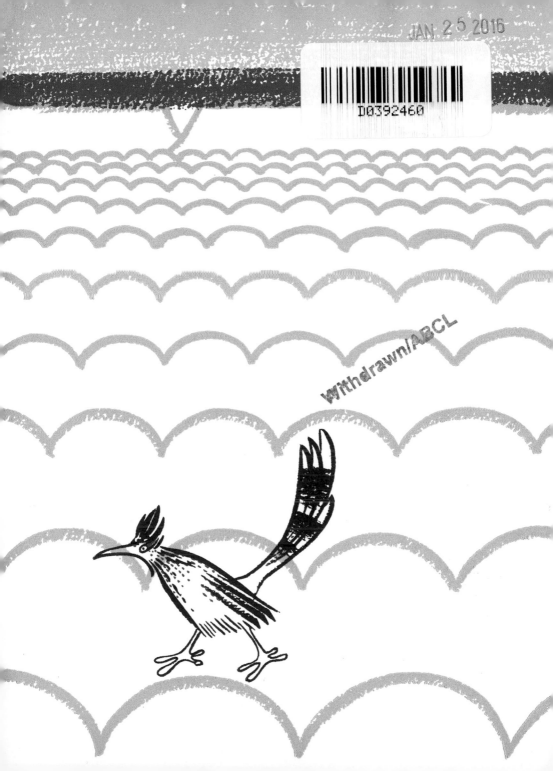

COCKY

Stories by LOYD TIREMAN

Adapted by EVELYN YRISARRI

Layout and Illustrations
by RALPH DOUGLASS

MESALAND
SERIES

A Facsimile of the 1946 First Edition
University of New Mexico Press   Albuquerque

2015 edition published by arrangement with Marilyn D. Carlson.
Printed in China

20 19 18 17 16 15   1 2 3 4 5 6

LIBRARY OF CONGRESS CATALOGING-IN-PUBLICATION DATA

Tireman, L. S. (Loyd Spencer), 1896–1959, author.
 Cocky / stories by Loyd Tireman ; adapted by Evelyn Yrisarri ; layout
and illustrations by Ralph Douglass.
     pages cm. — (Mesaland Series ; Book 4)
 "A facsimile of the 1946 first edition."
 Summary: "Saucy, strutting Cocky, a rollicking little roadrunner, joins
the baby jack rabbit Hop-a-long and the other animals of the desert"—
Provided by publisher.
 ISBN 978-0-8263-5606-2 (cloth : alk. paper) [1. Roadrunner—Fiction.
2. Desert animals—Fiction.] I. Yrisarri, Evelyn, adaptor. II. Douglass,
Ralph, illustrator. III. Title.
 PZ7.T5167Co 2015
 [E]—dc23
                        2015006376

COCKY MEETS HOP-A-LONG
FOR THE FIRST TIME

It was a bright sunny morning in the early summer. Hop-a-long had been down the arroyo, nearly to the village. There he had found a few tender grasses to eat. After enjoying a good breakfast he hopped along lazily, but was careful to keep one eye on the arroyo. The other eye was busy watching the banks.

Hop-a-long felt very happy. It was so nice to be full of food and enjoying the warm sunshine. Then he stopped. He stopped dead still. Because right there in the sand, before his very eyes, he saw the strangest footprint! It was the strangest footprint he had ever seen.—There were two of them!! Two footprints side by side, as though the stranger were walking. Hop-a-long sat down on his haunches to study them more care-fully.

The track looked some-

thing like that of a bird, but still it was an odd footprint. The strange part was that two toes turned forward and two toes turned backwards. Hop-a-long was certainly puzzled and said, "Is the thing coming or going?"

Then he thought to himself, "I might be in danger."

Hurriedly, Hop-a-long looked behind him, but saw no one. Then he looked right and left, but saw no one. Then as he looked in front he heard "Kr-r-rrt, what are you looking for, you long-eared, long-legged freak?"

Hop-a-long was so surprised! He could hardly believe his ears. When he saw the stranger he could hardly believe his eyes. Standing at the edge of the arroyo was the funniest looking bird he had ever seen. It was about twenty inches long, including its long tail. It had a coarse, ragged, bronze crest. The harsh, brown feathers were streaked with white. Its wings were short and it had a long bill.

This strange looking creature said, "You may as well look me over well. I'm going to be around here a great deal."

Hop-a-long remembered his manners. Although he didn't like to have this stranger call him a freak, he said, "How do you do? I am Hop-a-long, the Jack Rabbit. Who are you and where do you live?"

"I am Cocky, the Road Runner. I'm going to live here near the village,—that is, if you don't mind?" He stood with his head cocked to one side. He looked as though he were making fun of Hop-a-long and dared him to care.

"I am sure you can live wherever you wish," said Hop-a-long. "The people on the Mesa do not bother each other any more than is necessary to live." Hop-a-long wanted to ask more questions but was too polite. After all, maybe he could learn a great deal about the stranger if he kept his eyes open.

"Right now I'm looking for a cactus bed, or a mesquite thicket," said the stranger, "so Mrs. Road Runner can build a nest," and away he darted.

"Look at that bird run!" exclaimed Hop-a-long, in surprise. "Did you ever see a bird run like this one?"

The stranger was darting from bush to bush so swiftly that he looked like a brown streak. Every now and then he would give a sudden dart with his long bill but kept right on going.

"It looks as though he catches something and swallows it as he runs," said Hop-a-long. He couldn't see very well. "I better go and warn all the little folk of the Mesa about him," thought Hop-a-long. "The little animals must know about this new enemy and watch out for themselves."

Hoppy hopped along toward home a bit faster than usual. When he came out of the arroyo near the mesquite thicket, there was the funny-looking stranger.

"For goodness sakes," said Hoppy to him-himself, "this bird can run faster than I!"

That wasn't quite true but Hoppy didn't know it.

The stranger was looking at the mesquite thicket where Hop-a-long lived and said, "This looks like a good place in which to build a nest."

"Oh, no you can't do that. My family lives in there," said Hoppy, "but there are other places near by."

"All right. Anyway, this is too far from the village," said Cocky, and darted away after an unlucky lizard.

Hop-a-long sat down and wondered if he had been sleeping. The whole affair seemed like one of those dreams he sometimes had when he had eaten too much. "A bird with two toes in front, two toes behind, a long tail and bill, a bronze crest. A bird which runs instead of flying." But he had seen the stranger with his own eyes, so he knew he wasn't dreaming.

All over the mesa the other animals were having the same experience. They too, couldn't believe their eyes. And yet the funny looking bird was really there!

MRS. COCKY BUILDS A NEST

Mrs. Cocky was still looking for a place in which to build a nest. She knew exactly what kind of a place she wanted, but she hadn't been able to find it.

Some road runners build their nests in any kind of a place, but Mrs. Cocky was more particular. The place she chose would have to be just right. She wanted a home a few feet off the ground, with some shade if possible. Since she had searched the mesa near the village with no success, she decided to go up into the foothills. There she found plenty of good thicket but noticed there wasn't much food. So she continued her search back toward the valley.

Finally she found a nice spot in a mesquite thicket. It was about half-way between the thicket where Hop-a-long lived, and the village. It was also near the home of the Tumbleweeds. How happy Mrs. Cocky was, as everything seemed just right! She found several branches interwoven. By tying them together they would make a strong foundation.

The field mice who lived around there were not very happy about their new neighbor. Her habits did not please them at all. But there was nothing they could do to prevent Mrs. Cocky from building a home, as the mesa was free to any one who was brave and clever enough to live there. The field mice knew that all they could do was to warn the smaller animals. Of course, they must be careful themselves. The carefree days were gone now.

Mrs. Road Runner went to work at once. She gathered sticks about a foot long and carried them to the mesquite thicket. When there were no more sticks she began to pick up old dried cactus stems.

Mrs. Cocky had a stem in her mouth when she saw a lizard. Without losing a step, she swooped down on the defenseless little creature. By now the little animals were getting over their fright of their new neighbor and weren't so slow themselves. The little lizard darted off about as fast as the road runner. "Hurrah, a race!" said Mrs. Cocky, who dearly loved races. She ran after the lizard. Fortunately, the lizard was near his home and knew all the hiding places. Before you could say "scat" the little lizard had zipped into a crevice under a rock.

Mrs. Cocky had forgotten about the cactus stick she was carrying in her long bill. She picked at the lizard's tail, just as it was disappearing. The cactus stem broke in her bill and she missed the lizard's tail. "Fffttt!" said Mrs. Cocky in disgust. "I should remember that I can't carry sticks and hunt at the same time. I should either hunt or build the nest and stop trying to do both at once. Since Mr. Road Runner is waiting, I'd better stop hunting and build the nest. He might be angry if I keep him waiting too long." So Mrs. Cocky went to work on the nest.

Behind a bush she found an old snake skin. She cocked her head and studied it. She finally decided to take the skin. Mrs. Cocky wasn't skillful at nest building like some birds. When she finished it looked more like a pile of sticks than a nest. Then she got in and turned around and around many times. By pushing the sticks around, the pile began to take the shape of a nest. At least it would hold eggs so they wouldn't roll out.

Now Mrs. Cocky decided it was time to show Mr. Road Runner their new home. When he saw the nest he wasn't very pleased. "Oh, Mrs. Cocky, couldn't you get some grass and line it? I don't think you will like sitting on hard, sharp sticks all the time."

"A good idea. I'll line it," said Mrs. Cocky. She went to work picking up feathers, mesquite pods and twigs for the lining.

Then one wonderful day came. Cocky came back to the nest to find a buffy-white egg! This made him very happy. He knew then that Mrs. Road Runner liked her nest. Now he had a real home.

The warm days of spring were passing. Now the heat of the summer was coming to the mesa.

In the nest of Cocky and Mrs. Road Runner were several eggs. As yet there were no young birds. Every day Cocky would look anxiously at the first-laid egg, wondering how much longer it would be before it would hatch.

One day he rested in the shade of a nearby scrub-cedar tree. He was chuckling and crowing to himself. A bee came flying carelessly by. He jumped six feet into the air to snatch it.

Going back near the nest he heard a low, "perrp, perrp, perrp." It sounded something like a mother hen calling her chicks. He

hastened his pace. "Can it be that an egg has hatched?" he thought happily.

Yes, indeed it had. When he reached the nest, there was a baby road runner! My, it was an ugly little fellow! It had a blackish

skin with a few straggly stiff white bristles and a long bill.

But to Cocky it was the most beautiful baby in the whole big world. He was so excited! First he danced around the nest. Then he jumped as high as he could. Then he ran a short distance only to turn back at twice the speed. He crowed. He snapped his jaws to-

gether. He pumped his tail up and down
just as he does when you open and shut the
book quickly. Mrs. Road Runner watched

him calmly and quietly. She had seen him act like that before. But it was usual with him when the first egg hatched. After that first egg he didn't pay much attention to the others.

Finally Cocky calmed down and thought of more common affairs. He said, "The baby will have to eat. I'd better get busy and find something for it." He swept away in a burst of speed to look for a young lizard. It would have to be a nice soft little one, not an old and tough grandfather. Cocky, with long, giant strides, covered the ground with utmost ease. His eyes had never been sharper. For some reason, lizards did not seem to be very plentiful around there. Then he remembered that Mrs. Road Runner had been hunting near her nest for some time. So he decided to hunt farther away.

Cocky saw a slight movement near a rock. Before the lizard scarcely had time to wake from his afternoon nap, Cocky was upon him. It was an old, tough fellow. Cocky swallowed it himself. He found several more but they were old and tough, so he ate them, too. Then he found one that seemed just right. He ran back to the nest at top speed with it. When Cocky nudged the baby road runner he opened his big mouth. Down went the lizard

into the big opening. The lizard was too long and the tail dangled from one side of the baby's closed mouth. What a funny sight that must have been!

Cocky called to Mrs. Road Runner, "Shall I bring you a nice fat mouse?"

"Oh, no," said Mrs. Road Runner. "I prefer to catch my own, thank you. You just stay here a few minutes and watch the nest." With that she sprang off and ran away.

Cocky felt quite important and perched on a nearby limb. He flicked up his long tail, and then he flicked it down. Then he pretended an enemy was near. He put on his fiercest look, with his crest stiffly erected. Soon he became tired of pretending. Forgetting he was guarding the baby road runner, he darted off a few steps to snatch up an ant. Seeing a bug, he was after it. A passing grasshopper attracted his attention next. Before he realized it he was out of sight, and was not watching the nest. "I better get back!" he thought and raced to the nest. But it was too late. A hawk had spied the baby in the unguarded nest. Cocky came in sight just as the hawk was rising from the nest with the little road runner in his claws. Cocky tried to fly up, but his wings were not made for upward flight. He came crashing down. The hawk sailed up into the sky and out of sight.

Soon Mrs. Road Runner returned. She found Cocky sadly sitting on the edge of the empty nest. He told Mrs. Road Runner what had happened.

"Well," said Mrs. Road Runner, "In a few days another egg will hatch. Then we will have another baby in the nest."

Cocky could not be consoled by such a thought and said, "It is my fault that the first of this nest is gone. If I had remained on duty the hawk would never have seen the little fellow. My feathers are so near the color of the mesquite that the hawk would have passed by. But the baby didn't have the protecting color of feathers to hide him."

Cocky hung his head in shame and sorrow.

"Well, never mind," said Mrs. Road Runner again. "Next time I will stay and watch the nest myself."

COCKY AND THE RATTLESNAKE

The field mice who made their home in the tumbleweeds were afraid to move these days. Another new enemy had moved near them. It was a lively young rattlesnake. He had made his hole in the edge of a bank just a few yards away. Perhaps he had moved there because he had seen so many field mice around.

Already he had caught a number of the little mice. If something didn't happen soon he would catch a lot more. The young field mice were fast enough to keep out of his way. It was the very old ones who were in the greatest danger.

Now road runners like field mice too. It was Cocky's habit to come along every few days and pick up a fat morsel. That did not make him a very good friend of the field mice. But soon something happened to change their feeling toward him.

One day, just as the long-tailed Cocky rounded the bend in the arroyo, he saw the rattlesnake strike a passing mouse. Up went the crest on Cocky's head. This meant he did not like what he saw. He gave a little "prrrt, prrrt," as much as to say, "What are you doing here in my backyard, old rattlesnake. I'll fix you for butting in."

The snake heard Cocky and,
dropping the mouse, hissed, "Go
on away, you funny looking bird."
But Cocky did not go away.
Instead he came closer to the
rattlesnake. The snake coiled
rapidly, then waited for the
attack that was sure to come from
the road runner. Cocky danced
toward the snake, with one wing
stretched out before him. He
almost touched the snake. The

snake thought he saw his chance.
So he lashed out in a sudden
lightning strike. But he only
struck the stiff feathers on Cocky's
wing. Now Cocky struck back
at the exposed head of the snake,
but the snake was too quick. He
drew back his head with a hiss of
hatred. Again Cocky danced
away only to return from the side.
As the snake turned his head
toward Cocky, the bird's wing almost brushed him. This made the
snake furious. He had not been
accustomed to having birds or
anything else dance up toward
him in this fashion. Most of the
animals were scared to death of
him and always ran if they had the

chance. He struck at Cocky again, only to receive a very hard blow on the back of his head. It made him dizzy. This time he recoiled more slowly. Cocky darted to the side and came in from the back, but the snake had turned his long flexible body and was still facing him. Again and again the road runner came at the snake. Again and again the snake struck at the bird.

Once in awhile the bird was able to hit the snake's head. As a result, the snake began to tire. He realized that this strange bird was dangerous. He tried to crawl to his hole. But the moment he uncoiled, his head was left unguarded and Cocky would give him a hard blow. So he just coiled and waited. This time when Cocky came up dancing the snake didn't strike at him. His head was too sore and his neck was too tired from constantly darting it in and out.

Again Cocky came in from the front. This time the snake was a little too slow in turning. From behind the protection of his stiff wing Cocky gave the final blow. The snake writhed and struggled. The last blow had finished him. He soon was dead.

Cocky had saved the little field mice that lived in the Tumbleweed Apartments from their bitter enemy the snake. Now he would have more for himself!

COCKY VISITS THE VILLAGE

Cocky could run almost as fast as any animal on the mesa. This made him very saucy. None of the animals ever seriously tried to kill him for food. Even the hunters were amused by his antics and forgot to shoot him. All this made him cocky by nature as well as by name.

One afternoon he wandered down to the village. He liked to watch the people and village life. As he came near a shed, a woman came out with a pan in her hands. He heard her call, "Come! Chicky, Chicky, Chicky!" At once all the chickens stopped scratching in the dust and ran toward her. She began to throw something from her pan to the ground. The chickens gobbled up whatever it was with gulps of satisfaction.

"That looks like food," said Cocky, "Believe I'll go over and have some." As the woman turned back into the shed Cocky darted across the road.

You can imagine how surprised the chickens were. A stranger in their feeding pen! At first they started to cluck and run in alarm. Then an old hen stopped them by remarking,

"He is just a new kind of a rooster." It was true that he did look something like a rooster with his long tail. But no rooster ever had a bill like Cocky's. The hens were rather stupid and didn't notice Cocky's bill. Anyway no one would leave that delicious food, unless he were chased away. So Cocky settled down to eat. It was very good—far better than anything he had ever eaten before. He continued to gobble with the hens.

Now this flock of hens had an old rooster of their own. He was a big, red fellow, and the victor of many fights. He had not been there when Cocky arrived. He had been behind the shed teaching some young chickens how to scratch for worms. He had heard the woman when she called the chickens, but there was no need for him to hurry. He knew that when he arrived the hens would step aside and let him eat.

Feeling his importance, he strutted around the corner of the shed. As he strutted, each step seemed to shout, "Step aside, my children!" Some of the hens resented his ways, but they couldn't do much about it. If they ever disobeyed he would give them a sharp peck on their heads.

He swaggered up and shoved himself into the flock. He began to gobble the food as fast as he could to make up for being late. After he had eaten awhile he stopped to stretch and crow. It was then that he noticed the stranger.

At once he swelled up with anger and outraged pride. He gave a loud, challenging crow. Then he shouldered his way through the flock toward the stranger. He'd show this fellow! Strangers couldn't eat here without his permission, and he had no intention of giving such permission. No, indeed! Instead, he would give this stranger a good trouncing.

Cocky had been very busy eating. He hadn't noticed the arrival of the big red rooster. And if he had he wouldn't have paid any attention. Cocky didn't know the big rooster was the master here. But when he heard the loud challenging crow he stopped eating. Looking up, he saw the big rooster. "The old fool," he thought, "he'd better leave me alone."

The red rooster had no intention of leaving him alone. No, indeed. He went right up to Cocky, and without saying a word, sharply pecked him on the head. The fight was on. Of course, both were good fighters. Cocky was swift, but the rooster had spurs on the back of his feet. The rooster jumped up into the air, giving Cocky a cruel stab with his spurs as he came down. Cocky jumped to one side and knocked the rooster flat with a hard blow from his long bill. The hens clucked, partly

from sympathy for the stranger, partly in pride that their rooster was such a good fighter.

It is hard to say how the fight would have ended. Just in the middle of it, the woman came out. She ran to the rescue of her rooster, as she was very proud of him. With her broom she gave Cocky a blow on his back. There was only one thing for him to do, and he did it. He ran away as fast as he could.

The vain old rooster thought he had frightened Cocky away. He overlooked the fact that it was the woman and her broom who had really done the chasing.

Feeling more important than ever he swelled up with pride until he almost burst.

Then he gave a triumphant crow;

> "Cock-a-doodle-do
> I'm stronger than a rock.
> King am I of all in view,
> I'm master of the flock!"

Cocky had hidden in a bush across the road. "Is that so?" he thought to himself. "If that woman hadn't come to help you, I would have fixed you, you fat old thing. Never mind, I liked the food. I'm coming back again. Then we shall see if you can drive me away."

MRS. COCKY BECOMES A DECOY

Cocky was feeling very happy again. Up in the wide shallow nest another awkward dark-skinned little road runner had hatched. Cocky was going to be sure that this time no bird or animal was going to harm this precious little fellow. No, sir! Either Mrs. Road Runner or he would stay close to the nest at all times.

The sun was just about to peep over the eastern horizon. Cocky, wanting to enjoy it, scrambled to the tip-top of the mesquite bush. He liked to greet the wonderful sunrises. Cocky stood on the top-most branches. There he fluffed his feathers and enjoyed the warmth of the sun after the cool of the desert morning. Then he began to sing in a low gargling voice

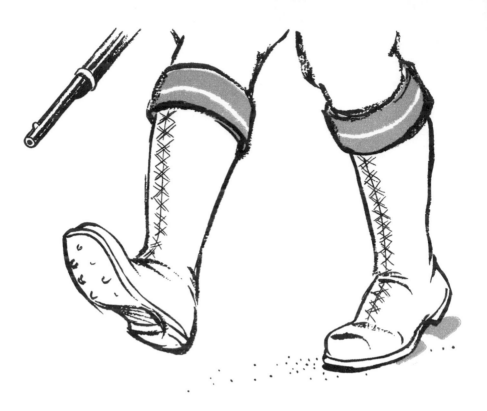

somewhat like a dove, "Koohoooo, Koo-
hooo." But it was soon time for less inter-
esting but more demanding business—that of
securing food for the baby road runner. So
he hopped down and started toward the
arroyo.

Near the village he heard the shot of a gun,
but paid little attention. It seemed to be far
away. Probably some hunter was after rab-

bits. Cocky caught an unsuspecting mouse. This he took back to the nest, and chucked it down the ever-ready throat of the big-mouthed baby road runner. Maybe that would satisfy him for a little while.

Cocky hadn't been gone long when Mrs. Cocky heard a "crunch, crunch, crunch," of heavy boots in the sand. She looked out between the branches of the bush. There she saw a man with a gun. She knew there was no danger for her where she sat, because her colors blended so well with the grass and bushes. The hunter could pass within a few feet without noticing her. But like all wild things, she feared the man. As the "crunch, crunch, crunch," came nearer, she became more and more nervous. She just couldn't bear for the hunter to come any closer to the nest. So she sprang out and down to the ground.

This startled the hunter. Without thinking, his gun went up to his shoulder. But fortunately for Mrs. Road Runner, his finger didn't tighten on the trigger. Instead he thought, "Why, that is a mother road runner. She must have a nest close by. Probably in the mesquite thicket." The man walked nearer, as he wanted to see the nest. Of course the bird could not know that he only intended to look at the baby road runner. When she saw him approaching she did a brave and unselfish thing.

Instead of rushing away at the top speed for which these birds are famous, she did just the contrary. She wanted to make sure that the hunter saw her. So she darted back toward him. Then she ran between two bushes where he could not fail to see her. She stopped and crouched with little mouse-like squeals to attract his attention.

The hunter saw her and knew she was trying to keep him away from the nest. He decided to follow her and see what would happen. He took a few steps in her direction. She retreated, dragging one foot, pretending it had been injured and that she couldn't go any faster.

Seeing the hunter's interest she thought, "Good! He is following me. My nest is safe."

Slowly she withdrew, managing to keep just ahead of the hunter. Now and then she would stagger a bit, then she would flap her wings as

if to keep her balance. This way the brave mother bird lured him away from her nest and her baby.

Finally, she decided they were far enough from the nest. The baby bird was safe now. So she gave one step and melted into the bushes. The hunter didn't follow her. He knew that if the road runner wanted to hide he could not find her.

"What a wonderful thing mother love is," he thought. "It fills the most timid with courage."